First published 2000 in *The Macmillan Treasury of Nursery Stories*
This collection first published 2010 by Macmillan Children's Books
a division of Macmillan Publishers Limited
20 New Wharf Road, London N1 9RR
Basingstoke and Oxford
Associated companies throughout the world
www.panmacmillan.com

ISBN: 978-0-230-75000-5

1 3 5 7 9 8 6 4 2

A CIP catalogue record for this book is available from the British Library.

Printed in China

MACMILLAN CHILDREN'S BOOKS

The Princess and the Pea

and other stories

Retold by
Mary Hoffman

Illustrated by
Anna Currey

The Princess and the Pea

There was once a prince who decided he must have a wife, but the only wife that would do for him was what he called "a real princess". However, he didn't seem at all sure what that meant. Still, as he searched for one, he became more certain about who was *not* a real princess.

The prince travelled from country to country and found lots of princesses but there was always something wrong with them. One was too tall, one had bandy legs, one ate nothing but salad, one had a passion for wearing yellow, one beat her servants, one read nothing but romantic novels.

It seemed as if there was not one princess in this world good enough to marry the prince and he went back to his own castle very disappointed.

Then, one night, there was a terrible storm, with thunder and lightning and torrential rain. And at the height of the storm there came a knocking at the castle door. The servant who opened it found a very bedraggled young woman on the doorstep. Her clothes stuck to her body and water ran down her pretty face and hair in streams.

"Please give me shelter," she said. "And, by the way, I am a real princess."

Everyone in the castle had come to see who was at the door on such an awful night. There she stood, calm and dignified and sopping wet. "Can this be a real princess?" wondered the prince.

His mother, the queen, had an idea of her own about that. "Come in and warm yourself, my dear," she said, and ordered servants to prepare her a hot bath and fetch her dry clothes. And while all this was going on, the queen had the best guest bedroom prepared in a most unusual way.

The bed was stripped and one dried pea placed on the bedstead. Then twenty mattresses were piled on top of it and cotton sheets and a big fluffy duck-down duvet. If the princess thought her bed at all odd when she came to get in it, she said nothing. She merely climbed the handy ladder that had been provided and settled down to sleep.

The next morning the princess appeared at breakfast with dark circles under her eyes.

"How did you sleep?" asked the queen.

"Very badly, ma'am," said the princess. "I'm sorry to say it but my bed was very uncomfortable. I felt there was something hard and sharp underneath me and I tossed and turned all night."

"A real princess at last!" cried the prince, clapping his hands. "Only a royal lady of the utmost refinement could have felt that pea under twenty mattresses."

And he went down on one knee and asked her to marry him on the spot. Perhaps it was lucky for him that she was not searching for a perfect prince. Anyway, what is certain is that marry they did, and they lived together all the days of their lives. And the pea was preserved in a glass case in a museum and, if it is still there, you may see it to this day.

Thumbelina

Once upon a time there was a poor young woman who longed for a baby. So she went to a wise woman and said, "I do so want a baby, just a little tiny one. Can you help me?"

"Of course," said the old woman. "Take this magic barleycorn and plant it in a flowerpot. Water it carefully and see what grows."

So the young woman gave her a silver sixpence, took home the barleycorn and carefully planted and watered it. Suddenly, a large colourful flower burst forth, like a tulip,

but with the petals tightly furled. The young woman was so pleased that she leant over and kissed the bud. Immediately, it opened its red and yellow petals and there, in the centre, was a tiny baby girl, no bigger than the woman's thumb.

"I shall call you Thumbelina," she cried, and was happy as can be.

The child had half a walnut shell for a cradle, violet petals for sheets and a rose leaf for her coverlet. She slept there by night and spent her days on the woman's table. Her mother had filled a plate with water and floated flower petals on it. Thumbelina sat on a tulip petal and spent the whole day rowing about, with two horse hairs for oars, on her own private lake.

One night, when Thumbelina was sleeping in her walnut shell, a large toad came hopping in through a broken window pane.

"That is just the wife for my son," said the toad, and took the whole cradle away in her mouth. She hopped out of the window and down to the muddy stream, where she lived with her son. As soon as he saw the little maiden, he said "Brekke-ke-kex, koax, koax!"—which was all that he could say.

"Don't wake her," said his mother. "Let's put her on a water lily pad. It will be like an island to her and she won't be able to escape."

How Thumbelina wept when she woke in the morning!

She had no idea where she was and there was nothing but water to be seen all around her. But she was even more alarmed when the toad and her ugly lumpy son swam up and told her she was to be married.

"We're just getting your bedchamber ready," said the old toad, and took her walnut-shell bed away.

Well, the fishes of the stream had heard the wedding plans and poked their heads out of the water to see the bride-to-be. And when they saw pretty little Thumbelina, they thought it would be a shame for her to have to marry the ugly toad. So they gnawed at the water lily stalk until it broke off, and Thumbelina went sailing down the river on her lily pad boat, far out of reach of the toads.

But still she didn't know where she was. All was well for a few hours, but then a large cricket flew down and carried her off. He, too, had fallen for her pretty face and wanted to marry her. But all the lady crickets said, "What an ugly thing! You can't marry *that*. It's only got two legs and no wings at all."

The cricket was sad, but he put Thumbelina gently down on the ground. Now she was alone in a wood, where she lived happily all summer, eating nectar from flowers and drinking the dew and singing with the birds. There was one swallow she was specially fond of, with his song of "Quivit, quivit!"

But when autumn came and the days grew colder, there was nothing for her to eat, and the dew was turned to frost on the ground. Even the birds flew away. Thumbelina was so cold and hungry.

So she left the shelter of the wood and crossed the cornfield, which was all stubble by then, and came to a field mouse's house. There she knocked at the door and begged for some food. The field mouse was a kindly old thing and welcomed Thumbelina into her hole.

"You shall keep house for me and tell me stories," she said. "And in return you can eat all you want. I don't think a tiny thing like you will be a heavy burden on my larder."

So Thumbelina lived with the mouse and told her stories and sang her songs and was happy enough. Apart from one thing. The field mouse had a neighbour, Mole, and she was always singing his praises to Thumbelina.

"He has such a handsome black velvet suit, don't you think?" she would say. "He's very wealthy, you know. You would be a lucky girl if he asked you to marry him. Of

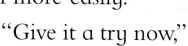

course, being blind, he can't see how pretty you are, but you can charm him with your lovely voice."

But Thumbelina didn't want to charm him. She didn't like him at all. Mole hated the sunshine and flowers and life above the earth. He liked cold dark tunnels and worms and piles of dead leaves. But he liked Thumbelina, too, and was quite interested in marrying her.

One day Mole told the field mouse and Thumbelina that he had dug a new tunnel linking his home to theirs so that they might visit him more easily.

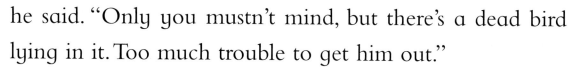

"Give it a try now," he said. "Only you mustn't mind, but there's a dead bird lying in it. Too much trouble to get him out."

So Thumbelina and the field mouse climbed the sloping tunnel to Mole's house. Halfway there, they came across the stiff bird, who was a swallow.

"Oh, poor swallow," cried Thumbelina. "You must have frozen to death. I wonder if you were the one who sang to me all summer?"

But the other two weren't at all sympathetic.

"See what all his squawking has brought him to," said Mole, who hated birds as much as flowers.

Later that night, Thumbelina crept back up the tunnel and laid a little blanket over the bird. She couldn't bear to think of him being cold. And next night, when she went to visit him, he opened an eye! He hadn't been dead at all, just fallen down in a frozen faint because of the bitter weather.

All winter long, Thumbelina brought him food and drink, and in the spring he was able to fly away in the warm sunshine. But with the spring came preparations for Thumbelina's marriage. Mole had proposed and she didn't know how to say no to him. The field mouse wanted it to happen and she had been a kind friend to Thumbelina.

Now the mouse insisted that Thumbelina should sew all her own linen and clothes and get married in the autumn. The tiny girl made this job last as long as she could for she certainly was in no hurry to marry Mole.

But at last the fateful morning of her wedding came and she went out of the mouse's hole to bid farewell to the

sunshine. She wept to think that, once she was married to Mole, there would be no more sunny days for her.

Suddenly, there was a call of "Quivit, quivit!" and her old friend the swallow was there.

"Why are you crying, Thumbelina?" he asked.

"Because I am to marry the horrid old mole and live

under the earth for the rest of my days," she sobbed.

"Don't do that—come with me instead!" said the swallow. "The days are getting cold now and I must fly south for my sunshine. I missed it last year. Indeed, I should have died of cold if it hadn't been for you. Let me save you as you saved me."

"All right then, I will!" cried Thumbelina, drying her tears, and she climbed on the swallow's back.

He flew swiftly up and away, and soon the wood where Thumbelina had been left by the cricket was just a dot on the ground and she couldn't tell where the field mouse and Mole lived. She snuggled into the warmth of her friend's feathers and let him carry her south.

It was a long journey but well worth it. The swallow landed on a tree in a beautiful

garden. The sun was shining with a full warmth that it had lost in the north, and brightly coloured flowers were in bloom.

"Where would you like to rest?" asked the swallow. "I have a nest in this tree, but it might be too high for you. Would you prefer a flower to sleep in?"

"Thank you, I think I should," said Thumbelina.

So the swallow swooped down to the ground with her.

And there, inside a red flower, she saw a tiny man, no bigger than herself! He wore a tiny gold crown on his head and had a pair of transparent wings. He was fast asleep, but woke up in some alarm when the swallow swooped down.

How he stared when he saw Thumbelina! He told her that he was king of the fairy people in that country and that

he had never seen anyone as lovely as she was. And Thumbelina thought she had never seen anyone as handsome as the fairy king. In fact, matters moved so fast that he soon asked her to be his queen. And since he was a much better match than a toad, cricket or mole, Thumbelina said yes.

The other fairies brought her her own pair of transparent wings and the couple were wed, with the swallow giving the bride away. And they all lived happily ever after.

The Twelve Dancing
Princesses

Once upon a time there was a king who had twelve daughters and they were all great beauties. He was very fond of them and didn't want them to leave him and find husbands, so he took great care that they shouldn't go out to parties and meet young men.

The twelve princesses all slept in one large bedroom and, every night, the king locked the door to it himself, to make sure they didn't creep out after dark. But here was a mystery. Every morning the princesses' shoes were worn to shreds, as if they had been dancing all night!

They wouldn't tell their father how this came about, and he was quite distracted. The king offered a fine reward to anyone who could find out where the princesses went dancing every night. If anyone did, he could choose whichever princess he liked to be his wife and become king in time, when the present king died. Each person who tried had three nights to solve the mystery but, if he failed, he would lose his life.

The prize was so great that many sons of kings came to try their luck but, alas, no one came near to discovering the princesses' secret. Then there came to town a poor soldier who had been wounded in the war and was no longer fit for service.

He decided to try his luck at the palace and see if he could solve the mystery. On his way, he met an old woman who gave him a piece of advice: "Don't drink the wine

that they will bring you at bedtime," she said. "And take this cloak. If you have the chance to follow the princesses, this will make you invisible."

The soldier thanked her heartily and walked on to the palace. That night, he was housed in a chamber adjoining the princesses' bedroom. The oldest princess brought him good food, better than he had tasted for months, and a decanter of wine. He ate a hearty dinner but he only pretended to drink the wine.

Then the soldier lay down on his bed and pretended to be fast asleep, snoring loudly.

The oldest princess looked at the soldier. "Here's another one who might have saved his life," she said.

Then she and her eleven sisters opened cupboards and drawers and arrayed themselves in their finest dresses. They were very happy, all except for the youngest, who said, "I don't know why it is, but I feel very strange, as if something bad were going to happen."

"Don't be such a goose!" said her oldest sister. "Just look

at that soldier. I hardly had any need to give him a sleeping-draught—he would probably have snored his head off anyway!"

Then she went over to her bed and tapped it, and it sank into the floor, leaving an opening to a staircase. The soldier watched all this through half-closed eyes and, as soon as he saw the princesses descending the stairs, he jumped up and threw the

cloak of invisibility

around him and followed them down.

As he hurried after them, he trod on the hem of the youngest princess's dress.

"Who's there?" she cried. "Someone trod on my dress!"

"Nonsense," said her sisters. "There's no one there. You must have caught it on a nail."

When they had all descended the stairs, they came out

into an avenue lined with trees whose leaves were made of
pure silver. The soldier broke off a twig and hid
it in his jacket. But it made such a crack
that the youngest princess was startled
and cried out, "What's that?"

"It must be a gun fired off in joy, because
we have got rid of our 'prince' so easily," said the oldest,
laughing.

They then travelled along an avenue
whose trees were made of gold and a
third whose leaves were all of diamonds,
and the soldier broke off two more twigs
to keep as evidence. Each time the
youngest princess started, but the others
took no notice.

They came to a great lake, where
twelve boats were waiting, each with
a prince sitting in it. And each princess
climbed into a boat with a prince. The
soldier slipped into the boat with the
youngest princess.

"It's strange, but the boat feels heavier than usual," said
her prince, straining at the oars.

At the far side of the lake was a castle all lit up with lanterns, and there was merry music coming from it. The soldier watched unseen as the princesses danced, each with her own handsome prince, till three o'clock in the morning.

Then the princes rowed them back across the lake and they walked wearily along the glittering avenues to the secret staircase. The soldier ran ahead of them in his magic cloak, so that he could dive back into bed, throw off the cloak and start snoring.

The princesses climbed back into their bedroom yawning and, when they were all back, the oldest tapped her bed and the staircase disappeared without trace. They undressed, discarding their worn-out shoes under their beds, as they did every night, and slept in late the next morning.

The next two nights were exactly the same. The soldier pretended to sleep, but in fact followed the princesses and their dancing-partners to the castle on the underground lake. And on the third night, he took a wine-goblet from the castle and hid it in his jacket.

After the third night, the soldier was summoned before the king. The king asked his usual question, but with no great hope:

"Where do my daughters dance their shoes to pieces every night?"

And the soldier replied, "In an underground castle with twelve princes," and he showed the king the three twigs of silver, gold and diamonds, and the wine-goblet from the castle.

Then the princesses knew that their secret was out and their dancing days over. The king told the soldier to choose which princess he would have for his wife.

"I am no longer a young man," said the soldier, "so I will take the oldest."

They were married that same day and the soldier was promised that he would be king himself, in time. But as for the twelve princes, they never saw their dancing-partners again.

The Magic
Porridge Pot

There was once a little girl who lived with her mother and they had very little money. The day came when the money ran out altogether and they had nothing to eat.

The mother sat weeping, with her apron over her head, but the little girl went for a walk thinking she might find an answer to their problem. And so she did, for wandering in the forest she met an old woman who gave her a little cooking pot.

Somehow the old woman had guessed the child's problem. "Whenever you are hungry," she said, "put the pot on the stove and say, 'Cook, little pot, cook,' and it will be filled with good sweet porridge. When you want it to stop,

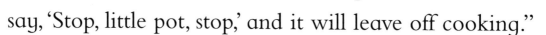

say, 'Stop, little pot, stop,' and it will leave off cooking."

So their problems were over. The little girl and her mother never went hungry. Whenever they wanted food the magic pot filled them with nourishing porridge and if they ever fancied sausages or doughnuts, well they never mentioned it.

One day when the little girl was out, her mother said the words, "Cook, little pot, cook!" and the magic pot started to bubble with porridge. When it was full, the mother wanted it to stop, but she couldn't remember what words to use. So the porridge boiled up over the rim of the pot and soon filled the whole kitchen. Then it poured right out of the door and down the path and still the pot kept cooking. It filled the next door house with porridge and the next and the next until the whole row of houses was

full of boiling hot porridge.

It was as if the pot wanted to feed everyone in the village. Soon there was only one house left that wasn't full of porridge and all the villagers were crowded into it.

At that moment the little girl came home. Or tried to. As soon as she saw the river of porridge running down the street, she knew what had happened. She ran to where the shape of her house could be seen under its overcoat of porridge and cried, "Stop, little pot, stop!"

Immediately the magic pot left off cooking and anyone who wanted to get back into their house had to eat a lot of porridge. The mother promised never to use the pot again, but I think she must have been a very silly woman not to remember the words to stop it, don't you?